KALLIE GEORGE (that's Kallie with an *e*) is an author, editor and creative writing teacher. She has written numerous books for children, including The Magical Animal Adoption Agency series, The Heartwood Hotel series, *Goodnight, Anne* and *Secrets I Know*. Kallie currently lives in Vancouver, British Columbia, and feels positively certain she and Anne Shirley are kindred spirits.

ABIGAIL HALPIN is an illustrator living in southern Maine, a few miles from the sea. Her illustrations are a blend of traditional and digital media, and she has illustrated many beautiful children's books, including *Fort Building Time* and *Finding Wild*. Her parents gave her a copy of *Anne of Green Gables* for her eighth birthday, which still sits on a bookcase in her studio, and her work for *Anne Arrives* was influenced by her teen memories of Prince Edward Island as one of the most beautiful, magical spots on the planet.

To all those whom Anne inspires — K.G.

For Sister Madeleine Marie — A.H.

With undying gratitude to L.M. Montgomery for creating the classic story on which this book is based.

Paperback edition published by Tundra Books, 2019

Text copyright © 2018 by Kallie George
Illustrations copyright © 2018 by Abigail Halpin

Tundra Books, an imprint of Penguin Random House Canada Young Readers, a Penguin Random House Company

Library and Archives Canada Cataloguing in Publication

George, K. (Kallie), 1983-, author
     Anne arrives / Kallie George ; illustrated by Abigail Halpin.

(An Anne chapter book; 1)
Previously published: Toronto: Tundra Books, 2018.

ISBN 978-0-7352-6573-8 (softcover)

     I. Halpin, Abigail, illustrator II. Title.

PS8563.E6257A83 2019   jC813'.6   C2018-903778-4

Published simultaneously in the United States of America by Tundra Books of Northern New York, an imprint of Penguin Random House Canada Young Readers, a Penguin Random House Company

Library of Congress Control Number: 2017952669

Edited by Tara Walker and Jessica Burgess
Designed by Jennifer Griffiths
The artwork in this book was rendered in graphite, watercolor and colored pencil, and completed digitally.
The text was set in Fournier.

Printed and bound in China

www.penguinrandomhouse.ca

1 2 3 4 5   23 22 21 20 19

Penguin
Random House
TUNDRA BOOKS

INSPIRED BY ANNE OF GREEN GABLES

Anne ARRIVES

ADAPTED BY
KALLIE GEORGE

PICTURES BY
ABIGAIL HALPIN

tundra

CHAPTER 1

One sunny afternoon in June, Mrs. Rachel Lynde looked out her window. To her surprise, she saw Matthew Cuthbert! He was passing by in his horse and buggy.

Matthew and his sister, Marilla, lived at Green Gables, next door to Mrs. Lynde.

"Where is Matthew going at this time of the day?" Mrs. Lynde wondered. "And why is he wearing his best suit?"

Mrs. Lynde knew all the comings and goings in Avonlea. But she didn't know about this one.

"I must visit Marilla and find out," she decided.

At Green Gables, Marilla was busy knitting.

"We have decided to adopt an orphan boy," she explained to Mrs. Lynde. "We need help on the farm."

Now Mrs. Lynde was truly surprised. "An orphan? But, Marilla . . ."

"The orphan is coming on today's train," added Marilla.

Mrs. Lynde did not approve.

"Mark my words, this is a mistake," she said.

 # CHAPTER 2

When Matthew arrived at the train station,
he didn't see a boy. But he did see a girl.

Under her old sailor hat were two red braids.
She had a pointed, freckled face and large eyes.
She was holding a worn carpet bag.

Matthew was very shy. He didn't know what to do.

The girl was not shy.

"Are you Matthew Cuthbert of Green Gables?" She stuck out her hand. Matthew shook it.

"I'm very glad to see you," said the girl. Her voice was sweet and clear. "If you didn't come, I was going to sleep in that cherry tree. It would be lovely to sleep in a tree. Can you imagine it? But I would rather go to Green Gables."

What could Matthew say to that?

"Come along," he told her.

 # CHAPTER 3

The whole drive back, the orphan girl kept talking.

"There is so little scope for the imagination in an orphanage. But here . . . Oh!" She gasped at everything she saw. And she made up names for all the places they passed.

She named the avenue the White Way of Delight. She named the pond the Lake of Shining Waters. The only name she didn't mention was her own.

Matthew was too shy to ask.

"I feel nearly perfectly happy," said the
girl. "But I can't be perfectly happy because,
well . . ." She held up a braid. "What color
is this?"

"Red," replied Matthew.

"Yes. I can imagine anything, except I cannot imagine away my red hair. It is one of my lifelong sorrows." She gave a great sigh. Then she added, "Am I talking too much? I can stop, if I try hard."

"I don't mind," he said.

Already Matthew liked this strange little girl.

But she was a girl, not a boy.

Marilla would not be happy.

CHAPTER 4

Matthew was right.

"Where is the boy?" exclaimed Marilla. She stared at the girl. "This is a pretty piece of business!"

"You don't want me?" The girl burst into tears. "Oh, this is the most *tragical* thing that ever happened to me."

Marilla sighed. "Dry your eyes, child. We won't turn you out tonight. What's your name?"

"Anne Shirley. Anne spelled with an *e*."

"What difference does spelling make?"

"Oh, such a difference," said Anne. "Anne with an *e* looks so much nicer."

Marilla sighed again. "Very well then, Anne with an *e*, it is time for supper."

But Anne couldn't eat.

She would have to return to the orphanage. As soon as she had seen Green Gables, she felt it was home. Now it wouldn't be. She was in the depths of despair.

That night, she cried herself to sleep. Not even the beautiful cherry tree outside her window made her feel better.

CHAPTER 5

In the morning, cheery sunshine poured through the window.

The cherry tree tapped its branches on the glass, like it was saying, "Good morning!" The Lake of Shining Waters sparkled in the distance.

Anne felt better.

"It's such a lovely morning," she said at breakfast. "But I like rainy mornings, too. Aren't all mornings interesting? You never know what might happen."

Matthew smiled.

Marilla muttered, "For pity's sake. I will tell you what is happening. I am taking you to Mrs. Spencer. Mrs. Spencer will return you to the orphanage."

Mrs. Spencer had brought Anne on the train. She worked at the orphanage.

For once, Anne had nothing to say.

After breakfast, Marilla and Anne went to Mrs. Spencer's house.

On the way, Anne tried to keep her spirits up. But it was hard. Especially when they arrived.

"Oh, I am sorry," said Mrs. Spencer, when Marilla told them about the mistake. "But what good luck. Anne doesn't have to go to the orphanage. Mrs. Blewett is here looking for a girl to take care of her children."

"Humph," said Mrs. Blewett, eyeing Anne. "There's not much to you. But you're wiry. I'll expect you to earn your keep."

Mean Mrs. Blewett wanted Anne to come work for her!

Marilla paused. "Well, I don't know," she said slowly. As stern as Marilla could be, she was also kind.

"Maybe we will keep her," Marilla told Mrs. Spencer.

"Did you really say that?" whispered Anne as she and Marilla walked home. "Or did I imagine it?"

"If you want to stay here, you must behave yourself, Anne," said Marilla. "And try to control your imagination."

"I'll try so hard to be good," said Anne. "It will be uphill work. But I will do my best."

# CHAPTER 6

Anne did all her chores, just like Marilla wanted. In her free time, she played and made up new names. Anne named the cherry tree outside her window the Snow Queen, and the flower on her windowsill Bonny.

"I don't believe in calling things names that don't belong to them," said Marilla.

"But don't you ever imagine things differently from what they really are?" asked Anne.

"No," said Marilla.

"Oh, Marilla. How much you miss!" said Anne.

Still, everything was going well. Until Anne's manners were put to the test.

Mrs. Lynde came over to meet Anne. She clucked her tongue.

"What a mistake! Didn't I tell you? She's terribly skinny, Marilla. Just look at those freckles. And that hair — red as carrots!"

Anne's face turned as red as her hair. "Oh! How dare you! You are a rude, unfeeling woman!"

Mrs. Lynde's eyes went wide.

Anne stomped her foot. Stamp! Stamp!

Mrs. Lynde's eyes went wider.

"Anne Shirley!" exclaimed Marilla. "Go to your room at once!"

CHAPTER 7

Anne lay on her bed and sobbed.

Marilla came up. "You must apologize," she said.

"I will *never* apologize!" cried Anne.

"You will stay in your room until you do," said Marilla sternly. "You said you would behave. But you haven't."

All that evening, Anne stayed in her room.

All the next day, too.

That night, Matthew tiptoed upstairs.

"It was awfully quiet without you at supper," he said. "Maybe you could apologize, for me? I've always wanted you to stay here."

Anne sniffed. "You really want me? No one has ever wanted me before."

Matthew nodded.

Anne took a deep breath. "For you, Matthew, I will."

"Just don't tell Marilla I said anything," added Matthew.

"Wild horses won't drag the secret from me," said Anne.

CHAPTER 8

The next day, Anne went to Mrs. Lynde's house with Marilla.

Anne was busy imagining.

She was imagining the best apology ever.

When they arrived, Anne threw herself down on her knees. "Oh, dear Mrs. Lynde, I could never express how sorry I am. Not even if I used a whole dictionary. Mrs. Lynde, please, please, please forgive me. If you refuse, it will be another one of my lifelong sorrows."

Anne clasped her hands.

"There, there, child. Get up," said Mrs. Lynde heartily. "Of course I forgive you. I am sorry, too. I always speak my mind."

"So do I," thought Anne.

"And," added Mrs. Lynde, "your hair is bound to turn into a handsome auburn as you grow."

"Oh, Mrs. Lynde!" said Anne. "You have given me hope."

Mrs. Lynde smiled. Then she said, "On the whole, Marilla, I like her."

So did Marilla. She smiled, too. "Good, because she is staying with us at Green Gables. Come on, Anne. Time to go home."

Anne's eyes sparkled.

Marilla and Anne walked back to Green Gables.

Anne slipped her hand into Marilla's.

"Oh, how wonderful it is to be going home and know it's home! Green Gables is the dearest, loveliest spot in the world. I love it already."

She had been Anne of nowhere in particular for as long as she could remember. It was a million times nicer to be Anne of Green Gables.